This Walker book belongs to:

Charles Dickens'

David
Copperfield

First published 2002 in *Charles Dickens and Friends*
by Walker Books Ltd, 87 Vauxhall Walk, London SE11 5HJ

This edition published 2014

1 3 5 7 9 10 8 6 4 2

© Marcia Williams 2014, 2007, 2002

The right of Marcia Williams to be identified as author/illustrator of this work
has been asserted by her in accordance with the Copyright, Designs and Patents Act 1988

This book has been typeset in Kennerly Regular

Printed and bound in Great Britain by Clays Ltd, St Ives plc

British Library Cataloguing in Publication Data:
a catalogue record for this book is available from the British Library

ISBN 978-1-4063-5695-3

Charles Dickens'

David Copperfield

Retold and Illustrated by

Marcia Williams

WALKER BOOKS
AND SUBSIDIARIES
LONDON · BOSTON · SYDNEY · AUCKLAND

Contents

Chapter One
My Birth and Early Life at The Rookery, Suffolk.

The afternoon before I was born my mother was sitting alone by the fire. She was poor in health and very low in spirits. My father had died six months earlier and she missed him sorely. It filled her with sorrow to think that he would never see me or hold me in his arms. Then the March wind suddenly blew open the front door and, without a word of warning, in marched my father's

aunt, Betsey Trotwood. She had come all the way from Dover convinced that I would be a girl.

"I am quite sure you will have a girl and I intend to be her godmother," said Miss Betsey to my mother. "Furthermore, I beg you'll call her Betsey Trotwood Copperfield."

Later that evening the doctor was called to attend to my mother. As the clock struck

midnight he came downstairs to tell Miss Betsey that I had been born.

"How is she?" enquired my aunt.

"Ma'am," returned the doctor, "it's a boy."

My aunt said never a word. She took her bonnet by the strings, aimed a blow at the doctor's head, walked out and vanished into the night like a discontented fairy!

Luckily, my pretty mother Clara was delighted with her new son, and named

me David Copperfield after my father.
We lived happily together, along with
my good nurse Peggotty, at The Rookery.
We were excellent friends and my
early years were very happy – until Mr
Murdstone arrived to darken our lives.
He was stern and handsome, and he began
to court my sweet mother – she was too
gentle to resist him. I didn't like him or
his ill-omened black eyes, and I don't

think Peggotty did either, but we were powerless to prevent his visits.

Over the following weeks my mother saw more and more of Mr Murdstone, so Peggotty and I spent more and more time in each other's company. One evening, as we sat by the fire reading my crocodile book, Peggotty made a welcome suggestion:

"Master Davy, how should you like to go along with me and spend a fortnight at my brother's by the sea in Yarmouth? There's the sea, and boats and ships, and fishermen and the beach. Wouldn't that be a treat?"

I was delighted by the idea and replied that it would be a very great treat. So, early one morning, we were collected by a man called Mr Barkis who drove us down to

Yarmouth in his cart. Mr Barkis took quite
a shine to Peggotty, as well as the hamper
of refreshments she had brought for the
journey!

Imagine my excitement when we arrived
in Yarmouth and I saw that Mr Peggotty's
house was a boat!

"Glad to see you, sir," said Mr Peggotty.
"You'll find us rough, sir, but you'll find us
ready."

I thanked him and replied that I was sure
I would be happy in such a delightful place,
as indeed I was. I found that I would have
a friend to play with: his niece, little Em'ly.
We immediately became the best of friends
and the days just flew by.

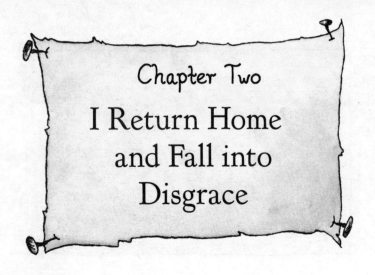

Chapter Two

I Return Home
and Fall into
Disgrace

When the time came to return home my
heart ached at leaving Em'ly. Only thoughts
of seeing my mother stopped me from
crying. But when I got home I found, to my
dismay, that Mr Murdstone had married
my mother! My new father would not even
permit my dear mama to leave her chair to
come and kiss me.

"Now, Clara, my dear," said Mr Murdstone. "Recollect, control yourself, always control yourself! Davy boy, how do you do?"

I did not do well at all, for everything had changed. My dear old bedroom had been moved, the empty kennel was filled with Mr Murdstone's snarling dog and – worst of all – Mr Murdstone's sister came to stay.

Miss Murdstone took the larder and storeroom keys from my mother and

began to run the household. She and
Mr Murdstone also took charge of my
education. They made me so nervous
that even though I was usually quite able,
I became unable to learn anything. One
morning, when I went into the parlour to
recite my lessons, I saw that Mr Murdstone
held a cane. The sight of it caused whole
pages of my lessons to slip away from me.

"Sir," I cried, "pray don't beat me! I have
tried to learn, sir, but I can't while you and
Miss Murdstone are nearby. I can't, indeed!"

It was to no avail. Grimly, Mr Murdstone
walked me to my room. He held my head as
if it were in a vice and prepared to beat me.
I struggled and he cut me. In a panic,
I caught his hand and bit right into it.

He beat me then as if he would beat me
to death.

Then he was gone and my door was
locked. I felt so sore, so sad and so alone.
As my anger cooled, I also began to feel
that I had been very wicked. For five days
I remained a prisoner in my room. In all
that time I saw no one but Miss Murdstone.
I longed to ask my mother's forgiveness,

but was treated as an outlaw and not permitted to talk to anyone. I think I might have gone mad if I hadn't found my father's old books to read.

On the fifth night, as I lay on the floor reading, I heard a whispering at the door.

"Is that you, Peggotty, dear?" I guessed.

'Yes, my own precious Davy," she replied. "Be as soft as a mouse, or the cat'll hear us."

Peggotty told me that I was to be sent to boarding school. She slipped me two

half-crowns, wrapped with my mother's love.

The following morning Mr Barkis came to collect me and, under the watchful eye of Miss Murdstone, I bade my mother, and my home, a tearful farewell.

Chapter Three

Salem House School

Salem House School was surrounded by a high brick wall, and looked very like a prison. As soon as I arrived, a placard was fixed to my back with the words: "Take care of him. He bites." written on it. It made me feel like a dog and made the other boys tease me.

Mr Creakle was our headmaster but not

our friend. He never spoke above a hoarse whisper and loved to slash us with his cane.

"You won't rub the marks out that I shall give you," he was fond of whispering.

There was only one boy Mr Creakle did not cane. His name was James Steerforth. He was older than the rest of us and extremely handsome. He quickly became my hero. He kindly took the money that Peggotty and my mother had given to me and spent it all on a dormitory feast! He had

great trouble sleeping at night, so he also kindly asked me to tell him stories from my father's old books – far into the night.

"We'll make some regular Arabian Nights of it," he would laugh.

The days dragged by in a blur of cracked slates, canings and tear-blotted copybooks. My only visitor was Mr

Peggotty who brought news of little Em'ly.

"She's getting to be a woman, that's wot she's getting to be," said Mr Peggotty.

I introduced him to Steerforth and they got on famously. Mr Peggotty invited Steerforth to visit his boat-home, which Steerforth thought most civil.

On the day of my birthday, I was summoned from the playground into

Mr Creakle's parlour. I hoped to find a hamper from Peggotty and I brightened at the thought of all the treats it might hold. But there was no hamper, just a letter. Mr Creakle sat chewing on his breakfast, but Mrs Creakle took me to the sofa.

"I grieve to tell you that I hear this morning your mama is very ill," she said. "She is dangerously ill," she added.

I knew all now.

"She is dead."

I broke into a desolate cry. I was an orphan. All day I cried and slept and cried again. I left Salem House the next afternoon. I had not been happy there, but I dreaded returning to The Rookery and the Murdstones.

Chapter Four
I Begin Life on My Own Account in London, a Lone, Lorn Child, just Ten Years Old

I remember little of the days before my mother's funeral, except that every night Peggotty would sneak up to my bedroom and sit with me until I slept. After the funeral, Peggotty married her suitor, Mr Barkis, and I was left alone with the Murdstones. Neither Mr Murdstone or his sister had any liking for me and neither of them knew what to do with me.

Eventually, they sent me to London to earn my living in the wine trade. My job was to paste labels on the bottles, cork, seal and pack them. I was only ten years old and alone in the world. My tears often mingled with the warehouse rats and filth.

Luckily, I lodged at the home of the

Micawber family, who were good friends to me. Mr Micawber was wonderful with words:

"If a man had twenty pounds a year and spent £19 6s 6d," he would say, "he would be happy. If he spent £20 1d, he would be miserable. Yes, Davy, procrastination is the thief of time. Collar him!"

Unfortunately, he was not as good with money as he was with words and was often

in debt. Yet the family always remained cheerful and however bleak their situation seemed, Mrs Micawber would always say, "I never will desert Mr Micawber!"

When the whole family was taken away to the debtors' prison, I visited them every day and shared my meagre earnings with them until they were released. Sadly, they then decided to make a new life for themselves in Plymouth. As I waved them off I felt desolate, for now I would be alone again. I returned to my wine labels and made a brave resolution – I would run away to Dover, to find my only living relative, Miss Betsey Trotwood!

Chapter Five
I Make Another Beginning in Dover

The following Saturday I gathered together
my meagre savings and possessions and
set out. My journey did not go smoothly,
and even before I had left London, I was
robbed of both my money and my clothes.
I remained determined not to return to
my old life, so I set off on foot to find my
aunt. It took me many hard days' walking

to reach Dover. I scavenged what food I could along the way and spent my nights under haystacks or in hop fields until at last I neared my aunt's house – footsore and ragged, unwashed and with my clothes torn.

My aunt was outside, guarding her lawn from donkeys. I stole up beside her and touched her softly with my finger.

"If you please, ma'am," I began.

She started and looked up.

"If you please, Aunt, I am your nephew."

"Oh, Lord!" said my aunt, and she sat flat down on the garden path!

When I started to cry my aunt took me indoors to meet her friend Mr Dick, who was busy mending a kite.

"What shall I do with him?" she asked.

"I should ... wash him!" came the reply.

So a bath was heated and I was washed and then trussed up like a bird

in clothes belonging to Mr Dick, who was considerably larger than I was!

"Mercy upon us!" said my aunt when she saw me, which in no way relieved my anxiety about being sent back to the Murdstones.

However, after a few days of rest and good food I began to feel very much happier, and quite at home with my aunt and Mr Dick.

Mr Dick was exceedingly fond of flying kites.

"It's a mad, mad world!" he would shout as the kite soared into the air.

My aunt, on the other hand, was exceedingly fond of chasing donkeys. The days passed most pleasantly, until one day

my aunt alarmed me by saying that she had
written requesting Mr Murdstone to call
on her.

"Shall I ... be ... given up to him?" I faltered.

"I don't know," said my aunt. "We shall see."

My spirits sank and I was terrified when
Mr Murdstone arrived, glowering at us all
with his ill-omened black eyes.

"Of all the boys in the world, I believe
this is the worst boy," he muttered darkly.

"Is he ready to go?"

"You can go when you like," declared my aunt. "I shall take my chance with the boy."

I could hardly believe my ears. I clasped my aunt around the neck and kissed her. I then shook hands with Mr Dick, who shook my hand back – a great many times!

"You'll consider yourself guardian of this child, jointly with me, Mr Dick," said my aunt. "And we shall call him Trotwood Copperfield – Trot for short!"

Thus I began a new life, with a new name and new clothes that were just my size!

Chapter Six
I Go to Canterbury and Am a New Boy in More Senses than One

Mr Dick and I soon became firm friends and would often fly his great kite together. My aunt also took to me kindly. She even encouraged me to believe that I might one day mean as much to her as if I had been the girl she had hoped for!

"Trot," said my aunt one evening, "should you like to go to school in Canterbury?"

I replied that I would like it very much, as

it wouldn't be too far from her and Mr Dick.

And so it was arranged that during the week I would board in Canterbury with Mr Wickfield, her lawyer, and his daughter, Agnes. Agnes kept house for her father as Mrs Wickfield had died. Agnes was my age and was very kind and wise. She soon became as dear to me as a sister.

My new school was not at all like Salem House. There were no canes and no masters like Mr Creakle. I studied hard and played

hard, returning home to my aunt and Mr
Dick for weekends and holidays. The time
seemed to pass very quickly and happily.

As I grew, I fell in and out of love and
confided each of my passions to Agnes.
She listened with great patience, but
never talked of any attachment she might
have. Indeed, I could think of no one who
deserved her. Certainly not Uriah Heep,
who was Mr Wickfield's fawning assistant
and the only person who ever gave me any

unease. Heep was a slimy schemer and one
of his schemes was to marry Agnes.

"I love the ground my Agnes walks on,"
he wheedled. "And she may come to be
nice to me because I am so useful to her."

Another of Heep's schemes was to take
over the business from Mr Wickfield.
His fawning ways drove Mr Wickfield
to drink, and before long he had made
Heep a partner. By a strange twist of
fate, Heep then employed my old friend,

Mr Micawber, as his clerk. Micawber thought no more of Heep than I did.

"His appearance is foxy, Mr Davy, very foxy!" he said.

When the time came for me to leave school and go to London to train as a lawyer, I left Agnes with a heavy heart. The thought that I was leaving my sweet friend in the same house as the awful Heep was almost unbearable.

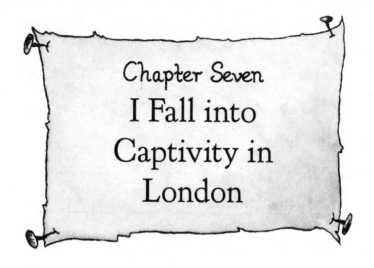

Chapter Seven
I Fall into Captivity in London

It had been my aunt's wish that I should
train as a lawyer and she paid for me
to be apprenticed to a London lawyer,
Mr Spenlow. I found the work dry and
dusty, and my heart was not in it – until
one Sunday, when I met Mr Spenlow's
daughter, Dora. All was over the second
I saw her and suddenly nothing mattered

but her. I was a captive and a slave. I loved Dora Spenlow to distraction. I thought I might also love her little dog, Jip, but he showed his whole set of teeth and snarled at me!

From that Sunday onwards my every thought was of sweet Dora. I wanted to marry her at once, but could not afford to. One evening I returned to my lodgings to find my Aunt Betsey, Mr Dick, a cat, two birds, the great kite

and a pile of luggage in my sitting room.

"I am ruined, my dear!" announced
my aunt.

My unfortunate aunt was bankrupt,
so she and Mr Dick had moved to London
to share my lodgings. Suddenly, I had to
earn enough money for us all to live on.
I decided to try my hand at writing,
which had long been a dream of mine.
I could hardly believe it when my first

story was accepted. At last I could make a living from doing what I loved, instead of being a lawyer! Eventually, I even managed to earn enough money to marry Dora and move into a new home.

How I loved my little wife. Our marriage started so happily, even though we were young and very bad at running our household.

"I'm such a little goose," Dora would say when dinner was late again.

Poor Dora. To my mind she was just not serious enough; she liked playing with Jip and strumming her guitar and I sometimes wished that she were more like Agnes, but my wise aunt encouraged me to accept Dora just as she was. This made us both

much happier and I believe we would have remained so, but then Dora miscarried our baby. She grew ill and weak after that and had to stay in bed.

"I am not very ill indeed. Am I?" Dora would ask me.

Yet her illness lingered on and when we were surprised by an urgent summons to Canterbury from Mr Micawber, I was loath to leave. Dora insisted that I accompany my aunt and only asked that I would hurry back once our business was settled.

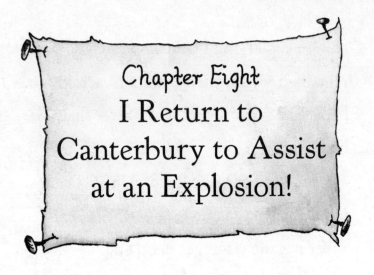

Chapter Eight
I Return to Canterbury to Assist at an Explosion!

When we arrived at Mr Wickfield's house, we were met by a very tense Mr Micawber.

"I trust you will shortly witness an explosion," was his strange greeting.

He then called for Mr Wickfield to join us in the office of the humble and fawning Heep. Once there, Mr Micawber did indeed explode!

"If there is a scoundrel on this earth,"
he shouted, "that scoundrel's name is Heep!
Mr W has been for years deluded and
plundered, in every conceivable manner,
to the pecuniary aggrandisement of the
avaricious, false and grasping – Heep!"

In his position as Heep's clerk, Mr
Micawber had discovered all the ways
in which Uriah had tricked Mr Wickfield
over the years.

"My services have been constantly called upon for the falsification of business," he continued.

It appeared that Heep had not only swindled Mr Wickfield out of his wealth, but many of his clients too – including my aunt. You can well imagine her fury! She grabbed Heep by his collar and shook him.

"You know what I want?" said my aunt.

"A straight-waistcoat." said he.

"No – my property," returned my aunt.

We demanded that Heep pay back every

farthing he had stolen, otherwise we would inform the law.

"I won't do it!" said Heep, with an oath.

But as soon as we mentioned the dark, damp cells of Maidstone jail, Heep quickly changed his mind.

With her wealth restored, my aunt wished to reward Mr Micawber for his part in bringing Heep to justice. She offered to pay for Micawber's family's passage to Australia. Micawber was delighted by the idea.

"It was a dream of my youth, and the fallacious aspiration of my riper years," he said. Although I very much doubt that he had ever thought about Australia in his life before!

Chapter Nine
Agnes

I returned to London to find that Dora
was growing weaker. Dear Agnes came
to visit her, but that night both Dora
and her beloved dog, Jip, died. I was
heartbroken at the loss of my child-wife,
even though we had often seemed at odds.
Then came more bad news, for I heard
that my old school hero, Steerforth, had

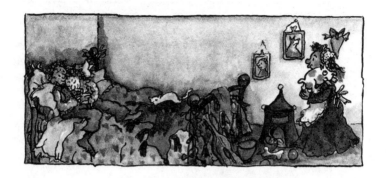

visited Mr Peggotty's boat home and
lured away his niece, little Em'ly, with
false promises of marriage. Filled with
these sorrows, I went abroad and stayed
away for three years.

In that time I came to understand many
things, especially how much Agnes meant
to me. She wrote often, but I missed her
terribly. I decided to return to England
to find out if she loved me. I went straight
to Dover where my aunt and Mr Dick

were back in their old home, chasing
donkeys and flying kites! Dear Peggotty,
a widow now, lived with them.

We were all four delighted to see one
another again. My aunt and I talked far
into the night and without disclosing my
intentions, I asked her about Agnes.

"Has she any lover who is worthy
of her?" I asked.

"I suspect she has an attachment, Trot,"
my aunt replied.

I decided to waste no time and to ride
over and visit her in the morning.

It was wonderful to see Agnes again.
Over the next weeks I visited her often,
but she never confided her marriage

plans to me. Eventually, I could keep my heart's secret no longer and told Agnes how much I loved her. To my amazement, I found she had a secret too: "I have loved you all my life!" she smiled.

Oh, we were happy, we were happy! That winter evening, we walked in the fields together and the early stars shone

down upon us through the frosty air.
Later we went home to tell my aunt,
Peggotty and Mr Dick of our engagement
and then we were all happy together!

We were married within a fortnight –
a small but perfect wedding. And as
we drove away, I felt that with Agnes
my life was founded on a rock.

Chapter Nine
A Last Retrospect

Agnes told me that before Dora died, she
had confided her hope that Agnes and I
might marry one day. Dear Dora, she knew
me better than I knew myself! Many long
and happy years have passed since then.
We hear that Mr Micawber is doing
well in Australia, as is Mr Peggotty,
who emigrated there with little Em'ly.

As for me, I have my friends and family close about me. Mr Dick plays with our boys and keeps Agnes's father company. My aunt spoils our little daughter, named Betsey Trotwood in her honour. My old

nurse, Peggotty, wears stronger spectacles, but still cares for us all and reads the children stories from my old crocodile book. And always by my side is Agnes – steadfast and true. Oh my Agnes, I have your love to guide me through the years to come.

THE END

Charles Dickens

Charles Dickens was a respected novelist who lived in Victorian England. He went to various schools until he started work aged fifteen – although he spent an unhappy period labouring in a factory when he was twelve. He wrote fourteen novels and many other shorter stories, becoming the most famous writer of the time. He died in 1870.

What the Dickens!

Marcia Williams

Marcia Williams' mother was a novelist and her father a playwright, so it's not surprising that Marcia ended up an author herself. Her distinctive comic-strip style goes back to her schooldays in Sussex and the illustrated letters she sent home to her parents overseas.

Although she never trained formally as an artist, she found that motherhood, and the time she spent later as a nursery school teacher, inspired her to start writing and illustrating children's books.

Marcia's books bring to life some of the world's all-time favourite stories and some colourful historical characters. Her hilarious retellings and clever observations will have children laughing out loud and coming back for more!

Books in this series

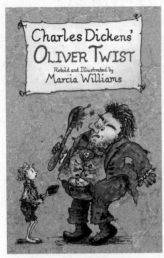

ISBN 978-1-4063-5692-2

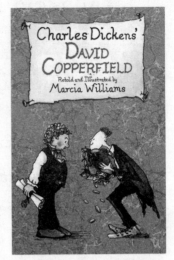

ISBN 978-1-4063-5695-3

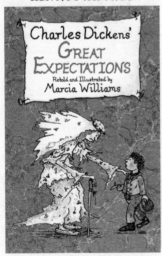

ISBN 978-1-4063-5693-9

ISBN 978-1-4063-5694-6

Available from all good booksellers

www.walker.co.uk